To Pippa Gerrett and Year Four (2004)
of Sturminster Marshall First School,
where this story began —JJ

For Suzy, with love —LC

First American edition published in 2007 by Carolrhoda Books, Inc.
Published by arrangement with Hodder Children's Books, a division of
Hachette Children's Books, London, England

Text copyright © 2007 by Julia Jarman
Illustrations copyright © 2007 by Lynne Chapman

Carolrhoda Books, Inc.
A division of Lerner Publishing Group
241 First Avenue North
Minneapolis, MN 55401 U.S.A.

Website address: www.lernerbooks.com

Library of Congress Cataloging-in-Publication Data

Jarman, Julia.
   Class Two at the zoo / by Julia Jarman ; illustrations by Lynne Chapman. — 1st American ed.
      p.   cm.
   Summary: While the students and teachers of Class Two are absorbed in looking at various
zoo animals, a sneaky anaconda gobbles them up, until Molly sees what is happening and
saves the day.
   ISBN-13: 978–0–8225–7132–2 (lib. bdg. : alk. paper)
   ISBN-10: 0–8225–7132–3 (lib. bdg. : alk. paper)
   [1. Zoos—Fiction. 2. Anaconda—Fiction. 3. Snakes—Fiction.
4. School field trips—Fiction. 5. Humorous stories. 6. Stories in
rhyme.] I. Chapman, Lynne, 1960- ill. II. Title. III. Title:
Class 2 at the zoo.
PZ8.3.J2746Cla 2007
[E] —dc22   2006030243

Printed and bound in China
1 2 3 4 5 6—OS—12 11 10 09 08 07

Class Two at the Zoo

by Julia Jarman
illustrations by Lynne Chapman

CAROLRHODA BOOKS, INC. MINNEAPOLIS · NEW YORK

On the day Class Two went to the zoo,
they saw a koala kissing a kangaroo.

They saw a giraffe
having a laugh.

They didn't see . . .

...the anaconda. zzzzz

They heard Teacher say,
"We must keep together!"
"Don't wander off!" and
"Watch the weather!"

They saw parrots
squabbling in the sky,
but they didn't see . . .

...the anaconda sigh
and open one eye
to spy on Class Two as they
walked through the zoo.

They saw hippos **hopPing** in the dirt.

They saw monkeys eating **chocolate dessert.**
But they didn't see
the anaconda ponder . . .

...after Class Two
on their trip through the zoo,
some of them walking **two** by **two.**

They saw spotted cheetahs running a mile.

They saw two gorillas **jumPing** a stile.

But they failed to see that **huge** reptile . . .

...open his jaws and swallow Kyle.

They didn't see that **giant** snake...

...add **Diana** to his feast.

They didn't see that greedy eater . . .

MONKEYS LEMURS

PENGUINS

. . . gulp down **Gerty and Anita.**

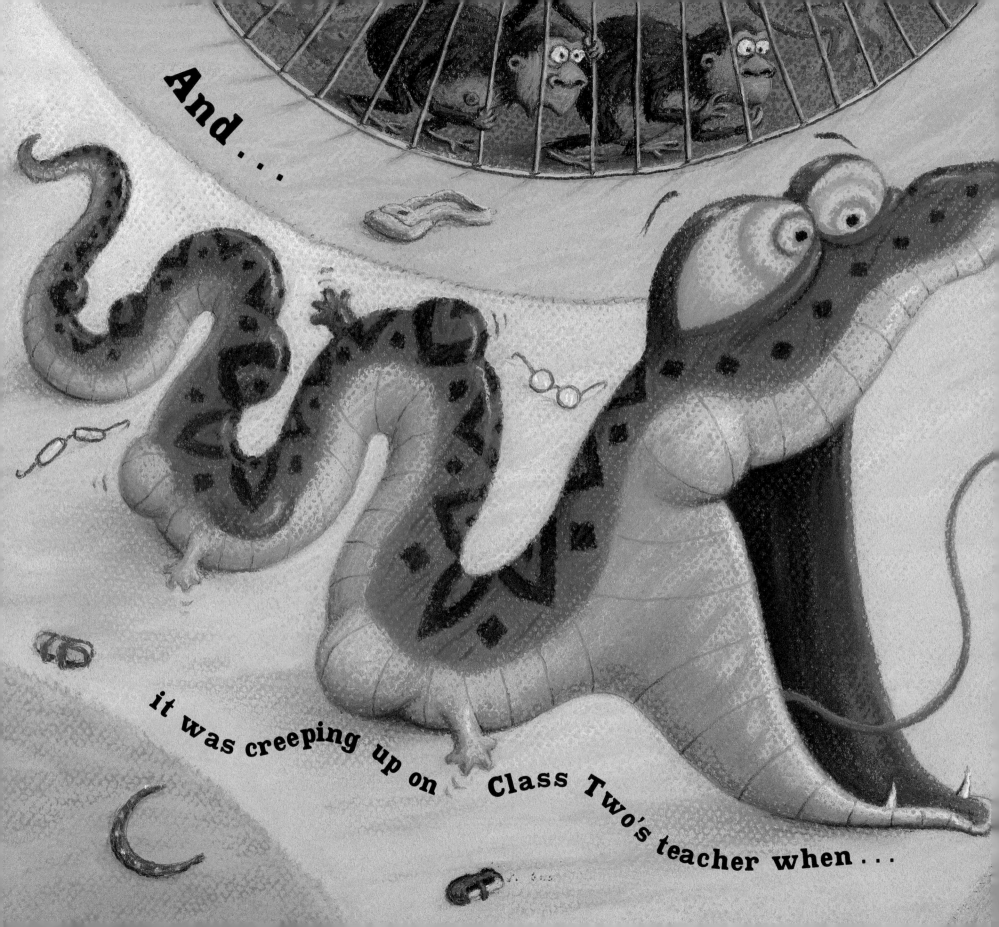

And...

it was creeping up on Class Two's teacher when...

Molly turned and saw the creature!

"**Look out!**" she cried— alas, too late. Teacher was gone and so was **Kate!**

Well, most of **Kate**—so **Molly** was quick.

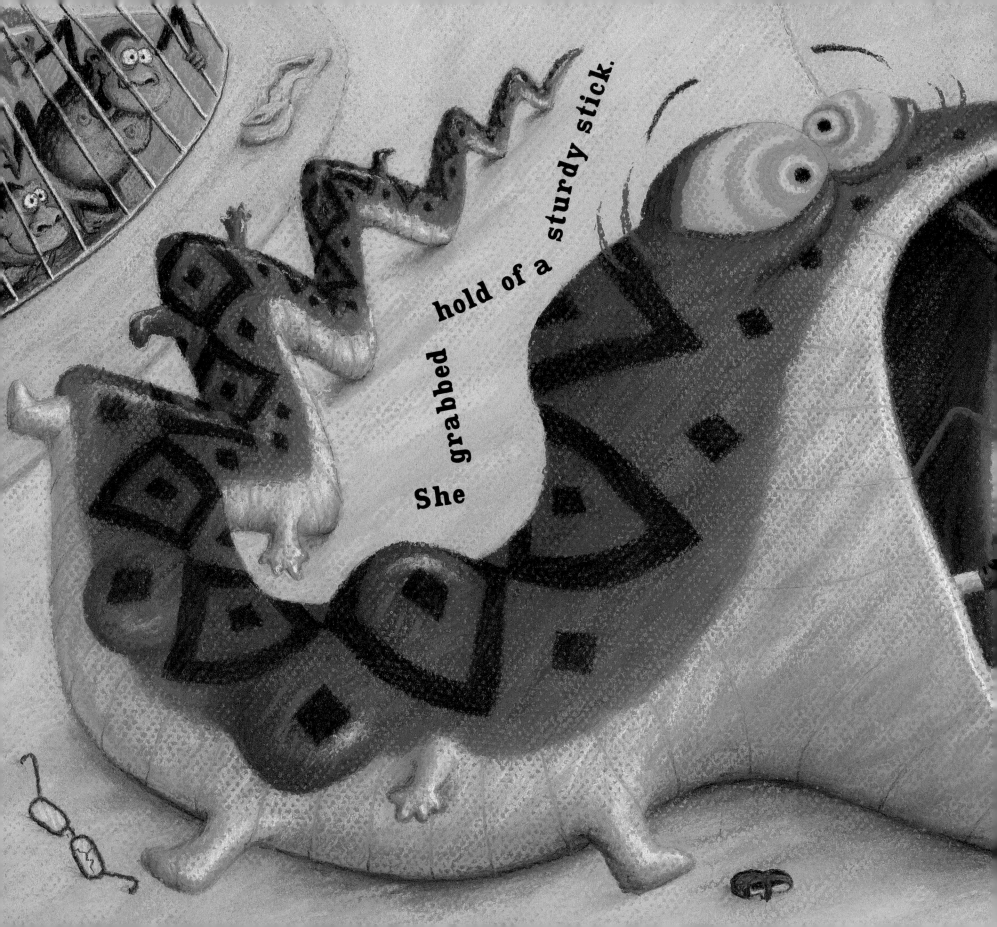

She grabbed hold of a sturdy stick.

Without a single moment's pause,
she stuck it between the
monster's jaws.

"Come on!"
she urged the rest of Class Two
as she grabbed Kate's feet,

**"To the
rescue!"**

The rest of Class Two all heaved and tugged . . .

and Gerty

and Anita,

and Diana

and Jake,

and James

and Kyle—

his smile
as wide as
a crocodile!

Then a boy they didn't know.

"Thank you," he said,

"my name is Joe."

"Phew!" said Class Two as they fled from the zoo.

Let this be a terrible warning for you!

If ever you go on a safari or visit a zoo,
keep your eyes open, whatever you do.

Watch out for the snake,
lying low in the lake.
And if you see the anaconda
open an eye and start to wander,
don't even for a second ponder . . .

. . . run!